SIMPI
Harmonica

hinkler

Steve Williams

Thank you to
Paris Cat

Published by Hinkler Books Pty Ltd
45–55 Fairchild Street
Heatherton Victoria 3202 Australia
www.hinkler.com.au

hinkler

Author: Steve Williams
Editor: Louise Coulthard
Art Director: Silvana Paolini
Photography: Ned Meldrum

ISBN 978 1 4889 4483 3

Printed and bound in China

CONTENTS

INTRODUCTION

This book is designed with the aspiring harmonica player or complete beginner in mind. You may not have even held a harmonica, let alone blown into one.

The aim of *Simply Harmonica* is to teach you everything you need to know to make those wonderful harmonica sounds come alive in your hands (or should that be lips?).

There is very little musical theory in this book. There are a few technical aspects you will need to learn to play well, but you certainly won't be required to learn how to read music.

In the coming pages, you'll learn about topics such as clean single notes, chords, note bending, vocal and wah-wah effects, microphone techniques and hot licks. You will learn the fundamentals of good blues and country-style harmonica playing, which will hopefully launch you on the way to playing the blues straight away.

By following the simple exercises, and with a bit of practice (and I know you're going to practise because you love the sound of the harmonica!), you'll find yourself wailing like a pro in no time. Practise the exercises, analysing and slowly repeating each part until you understand it, and then work up to a faster speed, just as you would in a face-to-face music lesson.

Good luck, and let's get playing!

PARTS OF THE HARMONICA

It's time to familiarise yourself with the harp. You'll notice that the notes are numbered 1 to 10 from the left on the metal cover of the harmonica. Number 1 is the lowest note; number 10 the highest.

Diatonic
harmonica

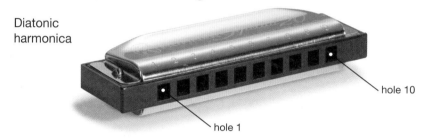

hole 10

hole 1

top and
bottom
covers

top and bottom
reed plates

body
(assembled
reed plates and
divider)

slide
button

12 hole chromatic
harmonica

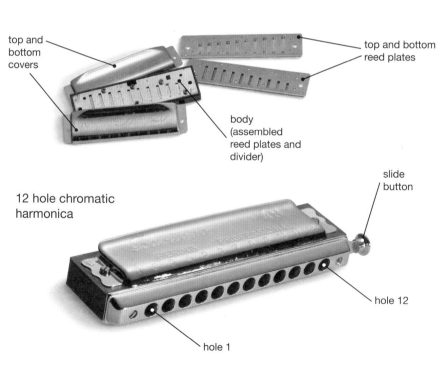

hole 12

hole 1

Types of Harmonica

There are two basic types of harmonica that make that sound you're probably familiar with.

The chromatic
Chromatic means all of the possible notes there are.

The diatonic
Diatonic means the notes of only one major scale.

The chromatic harmonica

The chromatic harmonica is larger than the diatonic and has a button on the side. It comes in 10-, 12- and 16-hole models.

The button allows you to play every single note in the chromatic scale. There are 12 notes in the chromatic scale. This is because it was decided centuries ago that the octave could be divided into 12 equal parts. Each of these 12 parts is called a *semitone*. A *tone* consists of two semitones.

All major scales are made up as follows:

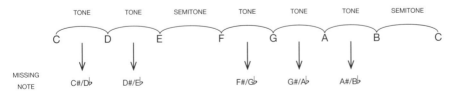

There is no semitone between the 3rd and 4th and the 7th and 8th scale degrees. This comes from the original decision to divide 8 notes into 12 semitones. The terms *sharp* and *flat* are used to name the semitones between the two tones. For example, the space between C and D is a tone. There is only one semitone between them.

- **Going up** from C, it is called C **sharp** (#).
- **Going down** from D, it is called D **flat** (♭).

C# and D♭ are therefore the **same note**. If you **raise** a note by a semitone, it is **sharpened**. If you **lower** a note by a semitone, it is **flattened**.

Here is the complete chromatic scale:

NOTE NAME	C	C#/D♭	D	D#/E♭	E	F	F#/G♭	G	G#/A♭	A	A#/B♭	B	C	START AGAIN
SCALE DEGREE	1	2	3	4	5	6	7	8	9	10	11	12	13	

When you get back to B, you just start over again in the next octave, and then the next one and the next: all using the same twelve notes. That's all the notes there are in all Western music. Every symphony and every rock and roll, blues, country and western and rap song is made from those 12 notes.

This means that the chromatic harmonica is just like most other musical instruments. You need to learn all the scales in every key. That's probably why there are relatively few chromatic harmonica players. It's a difficult instrument to master.

The chromatic harmonica was a very popular instrument up until the late 1940s. It was used in classical music as well as in a variety of jazz styles. Some great players from that era include Larry Adler and Max Geldray.

In the modern era, Stevie Wonder and Norton Buffalo are some of the greats. With the advent of rock and roll in the 50s and 60s, which was heavily influenced by the blues, the chromatic harmonica began to disappear from widespread use. It was replaced by the more recognisable bluesy wailing sound of the small ten-hole diatonic harmonica.

THE DIATONIC HARMONICA

The harmonica that produces just about all the blues- and country-style sounds is the diatonic. It is also known as the blues harp.

The 10-hole diatonic harmonica, or harp, comes in twelve keys: one for each note of the chromatic scale. The advantage of this is that, unlike the chromatic harmonica on which you must learn every key and every scale, with the diatonic you can simply change harps to play in another key.

The techniques and tricks you learn on a harp in one key are applicable to all the other diatonic harps in the other keys. That is why the blues harp is such an easy instrument to learn. In fact, it is 12 times easier to learn than any other instrument! But which one should you get?

Some harmonicas have wooden reed dividers that can move about or swell up with moisture. This can cause the lips to shred, so it's best to stick to harps that have plastic dividers between the reeds. These days, most harmonicas are made with the plastic dividers.

If you want to play along with a guitar or you're hoping to jam with a band, you'll probably need half a dozen different key harmonicas in the most common rock and blues keys.

The exercises in this book are performed on a C harp. This is because there are no sharps or flats in the key of C, which makes discussing the techniques less complicated. However, because we are mostly discussing which holes to play instead of which notes, the exercises are applicable to any key harmonica.

HOLDING THE HARMONICA

Hold the harmonica in your left hand between the thumb and the forefinger. It's pretty much like holding a sandwich, with your index finger right in the middle of the top metal cover. The low notes are to the left.

Some players hold the harmonica the other way around, with the low notes to the right. The famous country blues man Sonny Terry played this way. It can depend on how you first began playing, but the most common method is with the low notes to the left.

Holding the harp in your left hand leaves your right hand free to make all sorts of cupping and wah-wah effects.

When you are playing harp with a microphone through an amplifier or a P.A. system, hold the harmonica with your left hand but hold the microphone as well. The right hand can act as a support because there are fewer hand effects used when playing amplified harmonica.

Holding a harmonica and a microphone

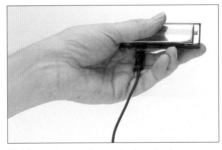

Holding a harmonica and a lapel mike

LAYOUT OF THE NOTES

The layout of the notes on a C harmonica.

There are two sets of metal reeds in a harmonica. The top reeds respond when you **blow**. The bottom reeds respond when you suck or **draw** air through them.

When you are told to draw 2, it means to suck, or draw, on hole 2. If you are told to blow 6, it to means blow on hole 6.

There is only one complete major scale on the diatonic harmonica. It begins on blow 4 and finishes on blow 7. On a C harmonica this is a C major scale, on a D harmonica it's the D major scale, on a G harmonica it's the G major scale, and so on.

This is why the harmonica is such an easy instrument to play. All the notes are laid out in exactly the same relationship to each other, so once you've learned a lick in one key, you can play that lick in a different key just by picking up a harmonica in that key.

If you want to play traditional melodies such as *Row, Row, Row Your Boat,* this is the part of the harmonica that you will use. It is called **first position**, **straight-harp** or **melody-style** harmonica.

Blues and country harmonica are not played in this first position. These styles are played in what is known as cross harp or second position, which will be addressed later.

HARMONICA NOTATION

L et's explore the standard notation system for harp riffs and tunes.

- The number indicates **which hole to play**.
- The up arrow means **blow** (think of it as 'blow up').
- The down arrow means **draw** (think of it as 'draw down').

So a C major scale played on a C harp in first position reads as follows:

C	D	E	F	G	A	B	C
4	4	5	5	6	6	7	7
↑	↓	↑	↓	↑	↓	↓	↑
BLOW	DRAW	BLOW	DRAW	BLOW	DRAW	DRAW	BLOW

Some notes on the harp have to be played by bending the air stream over the reed. This vital technique is discussed on page 24.

On holes 1, 4 and 6 there is only one bend available.

On hole 3, there are three available bent notes.

It is indicated by a curved arrow.

The first bent note on hole 3 is indicated by a cut-curved arrow.

On hole 2, there are two bent notes.

The first bent note on hole 2 is indicated by a cut-curved arrow.

The second bent note on hole 3 is indicated by a curved arrow with two cuts.

The second bent note on hole 2 is indicated by a curved arrow with two cuts.

The third bent note on hole 3 is indicated by a curved arrow with three cuts.

PUCKERING UP

When you buy your first harmonica, there may be a little instructional piece of paper with it that shows you how to play. It may say to open your mouth up about four holes wide and block off three holes with your tongue. This is called the tongue blocking method of playing. It's great for playing old-fashioned first position melodies, but it's not what is used when playing the blues.

The tongue is very important in blues and country harmonica, as it is used for different sound effects, such as bending notes and vibrato, so we need to learn to **pucker up**.

This is the shape your mouth needs to make in order to pucker up.

The object is to get a clear, sharp tone from each single note of the harmonica. This is the single most important step in learning blues harp. Your breathing should be natural and not forced. Your lips should be puckered so that only one note emerges, clear, sweet and pure.

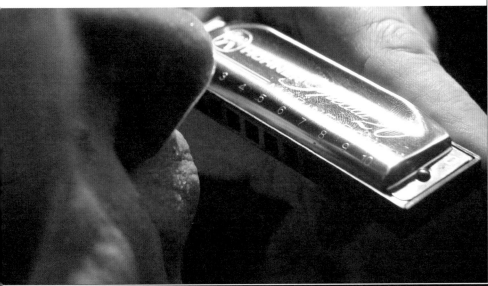

DRAWING ON THE FIRST FOUR HOLES

Exercise 1

1	2	3	4
↓	↓	↓	↓
DRAW	DRAW	DRAW	DRAW

repeat

1 Begin by drawing on hole 1. Make your mouth small enough to draw just that one note. Play the note over and over. Repetition is the key to getting the fundamentals right.

2 Next try drawing on hole 2. If you produce more than one note, try using your two index fingers to block off the other holes. This will give you an idea how small your mouth needs to be to get the single notes sounding clean and pure.

Using the index fingers to block holes

3 Now try hole 3, once again using your index fingers to block the holes if you cannot get a clean sound. Play the note over and over until you have a completely clean tone.

4 Draw on hole 4. Remember, every note we are playing is being sucked, not blown.

When you can produce a single clear note on the four holes, you are well on your way to developing the fundamental technique for playing blues and country harmonica.

Here are two exercises to practise drawing the single notes, puckered up, on the first four holes. Repeat these exercises until you can play each note clearly.

Exercise 2

1	2	3	4	3	2	1
↓	↓	↓	↓	↓	↓	↓
DRAW	DRAW	DRAW	DRAW	DRAW	DRAW	DRAW

repeat

Exercise 3

1	3	2	4
↓	↓	↓	↓
DRAW	DRAW	DRAW	DRAW

repeat

These exercises may look easy, particularly if you begin by playing them slowly. However, as you play them faster, you may find that they're not as easy as they look. If you persevere and build up your speed gradually, you will find that these simple exercises will lay the foundation for a great harmonica technique.

DRAWING ON THE FIFTH AND SIXTH HOLES

Once you have mastered the exercises for the first four holes, try drawing on holes 5 and 6. Repeat drawing until you can create a clean pure sound from both holes.

Once you have these two holes under control, build on the previous exercises by adding to them. Repeat these exercises until you can play each note clearly.

Exercise 4

4	5	6
↓	↓	↓
DRAW	DRAW	DRAW

repeat

Exercise 5

4	5	6	6	5	4
↓	↓	↓	↓	↓	↓
DRAW	DRAW	DRAW	DRAW	DRAW	DRAW

repeat

It may not sound very musical but focus on building the fundamentals for the time being. Keep practising puckering up and single note playing until it is completely under control. It is critically important.

DRAWING ON ALL SIX HOLES

Here are two expanded exercises using all 6 holes.

Exercise 6

1	2	3	4	5	6
↓	↓	↓	↓	↓	↓
DRAW	DRAW	DRAW	DRAW	DRAW	DRAW

repeat

Exercise 7

1	2	3	4	5	6	5	4	3	2	1
↓	↓	↓	↓	↓	↓	↓	↓	↓	↓	↓
DRAW	DRAW	DRAW	DRAW	DRAW	DRAW	DRAW	DRAW	DRAW	DRAW	DRAW

repeat

CROSS HARP

Just about all blues and country-style is played in a position known as **cross harp**.

Cross harp, or **second position**, is the technique of playing a harmonica in a different key to the key that the rest of the band is playing in. You are still playing in the same key as the band; you are just using a different key harmonica to get the right blues notes.

Cross harp is by far the most common style used in blues, rock and country music. It differs from straight or melody harp because the emphasis is on the drawn or sucked notes, not the blown notes.

It is easier to 'colour' the note when drawing, which means making the note bend or wail. Colouring the note gives the blues harp its distinctive and unique sound.

Here is a list of the most common rock and blues keys and the correct harp to use for cross position:

GUITAR OR BAND KEY	CROSS HARP KEY
E	A
A	D
D	G
G	C
C	F
F	B♭/A#

These are the keys you'll almost always be playing in. Serious harmonica players own harps in all 12 keys, so they can play with any band in any key.

Here are the remaining keys and the cross harp to use in those keys:

GUITAR OR BAND KEY	CROSS HARP KEY
E♭/D#	A♭/G#
A♭/G#	D♭/C#
C#/D♭	F#/G♭
F#/G♭	B
B	E
B♭/A#	E♭/D#

Harmonica makers mix up the flats and sharps, which is why both keys are listed. If a guitarist is playing in G flat (G♭), you need to know that this also means F sharp (F#), and so the correct harmonica to use is in the key of B.

Keep a little piece of paper listing all the keys and the right harmonica in your bag of harmonicas, so you'll always know the right harp to use.

Always check what key the band or guitarist is playing in. Not many guitarists know about cross harp. Don't forget, you're still playing in the same key as the band; it's just that the notes on a harmonica are ideally set up to wail the blues in cross position.

Here is an example, using a C harmonica. As discussed previously, if you **blow** into your C harp on holes 1, 2, 3 and 4 or holes 2, 3, 4 and 5 or holes 4, 5, 6 and 7 (or any combination really), you get a C chord and a C scale. This is perfect for simple campfire melodies or the tunes that a casual 'mouth organ' player might play. This is called **first position**, or **straight harp**.

But if you **draw** on holes 1, 2, 3 and 4, you get the notes D, G, B and D. This is a G chord. If you include the draw 5 hole, you also get the F note: a very bluesy sound. This chord is called a G seventh (because F is the seventh note in the G blues scale). Some clever player realised that if you mostly **draw** instead of **blow**, you are playing the blues in G on a C harp.

To summarise:
- old fashioned melody harmonica emphasises the blow notes and uses the same key harp as the key the band is playing in.
- blues harmonica emphasises the draw notes and uses a different key harp to the key the band is playing in.

All you need to do is ask the band what key the song is in and then count up 4 steps to get the right key harp.

For example:

- The band is playing in G.
- Count

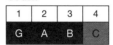

- Use a C harp.

- The band is playing in A.
- Count

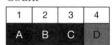

- Use a D harp.

- The band is playing in C.
- Count

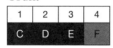

- Use an F harp.

Confused? Don't worry! All you need to remember is which harp goes with which key and which holes to use. Don't get hung up on the technical stuff, as eventually it will all make sense.

You will notice that all these notes are made by drawing on the various harmonica holes. This is why our first exercises were about learning to get a clean single note drawing on holes 1 to 6.

So now you can play a clean note on all the holes and you know which harp to use. Now all you need to learn is how to bend those notes and you will have all the fundamentals covered. You'll be wailing in no time!

THE GRAMMAR OF MUSIC

There is virtually no need to learn to read the standard musical notation system because there is no music written for blues harp. In a live or studio situation you will almost never be called on to read a piece of music for the blues harp.

In fact, it is not necessary to learn any musical theory beyond the principle of the cross harp and the basic chords of the blues. This is because the harp is what is called a position instrument. The licks you learn on any harp are applicable to every other harp. Unlike, for example, the saxophone, where to learn a riff in all twelve keys requires learning twelve different sets of fingerings, the only physical effort required with the harp is picking up the right one for the right key.

I've had students ask me if it is necessary to learn how to read notes on the page. My answer is that if learning to read music was so important, Ray Charles and Stevie Wonder wouldn't be successful as performers. Music is an aural art, not a visual one. You need your ears working, not your eyes.

Despite this, you still need to learn the grammar of music. Before you went to school, you probably couldn't read, but you could certainly talk. People with profound dyslexia can struggle to read, but they can speak perfectly fluently. This is because we understand the basic rules from a very early age: the grammar of speech.

The same thing applies to music. To learn how to play you need to understand how the little 'sentences' of music (the licks) fit together, just like words fit together in speech.

BENDING

Now it's time to bend. The crying, wailing sound you've heard on recordings is created by 'bending' the notes on the harp.

Why is bending so important? The answer requires some music theory.
- Draw on hole 2. On the C harmonica, that's a G note.
- Now blow on hole 2. That's an E note.

Between the G and the E, there are two other notes. They are the F# and the F natural.

Where are they? They're just not there. The diatonic harmonica has notes missing. The technique for playing those notes is called **bending**. Unlike guitarists, who physically bend the strings with their fingers, a harmonica player has to learn to bend the column of air passing over the metal reeds of the harp.

Changing the angle of the air flow causes the reed to vibrate at a different point along its length, producing a different note. The art of bending is very refined and eventually you should be able to get two separate bends from draw 2, three bends from draw 3 and one each from draws 1, 4 and 6.

This is easily the most difficult harp technique to master and unless you can get a clean sound by puckering up, you will not be able to make your mouth, throat and tongue do what's required of them to bend notes.

Here is a list of the holes and the bends which must be learnt and mastered in order to play the blues on the C harmonica.

HOLE	BLOW	DRAW	BENDS (MISSING NOTES)
1	C	D	C#
2	E	G	F#, F
3	G	B	B♭, A, A♭
4	C	D	C#
5	E	F	NONE
6	G	A	A♭

All of the bends listed above are on the draw notes.

So, to summarise:
- the diatonic harmonica has notes missing.
- there are two notes missing on draw 2, three notes missing on draw 3 and one note missing from draw 1, 4 and 6.
- these notes must be produced by bending the column of air passing over the reeds. This causes the reeds to resonate and vibrate at a different point and lowers the pitch.

Now, let's look at the technique in detail.

To bend, play a long, clean draw note on either hole 4 or hole 6. As you can see from the chart on the previous page, there is only one bend note that can be produced from these holes. (Hole 1 is the same, but it is the lowest draw note on the harp, which means the reed is longer and heavier and therefore harder to control at the beginner stage.)

1 Whilst playing a long note, think of how the air is simply passing through the harp and into your lungs.

2 Now think of the air being curved down your throat while your tongue arches slightly, with its tip down near the bottom gum. Drop your jaw slightly and tighten the facial muscles around the nose and mouth.

3 If it won't come, try singing a note you are comfortable with. Now lower the pitch and try to sing as low as you possibly can. Notice how your jaw drops and your tongue seems to lie on the bottom of your mouth. That's the basic technique. Now try it on the harp.

Probably nothing will happen. A lot more sucking force is necessary for bending and your tongue and facial muscles may not yet be strong enough to sustain the bent column of air. You may get a little short bend but the object is to get all the bent notes sounding as clean as the straight notes. This can take literally years of practice (well it took me that long anyway). You have to be able to hit the bent note by itself cleanly, by shaping your mouth the right way and not just bending down to the note from the clean draw note.

It really is a trick but once you've managed it, it will never escape your grasp. Just getting the first bend is the hardest part. If it won't come, try crying into your harp, screaming at it or getting angry with it. This may cause the position of the air column to change and bang! You've got it!

Above all, don't get discouraged. Getting your first bend can take a long time, but once you get the trick to work, you're on your way. If you have hours of frustrating failures, go away and do something else for a while and then come back and try again. The feeling you get from your first successful bend is fantastic and the rewards for all your practice and striving will be obvious.

Once you've managed to bend a note, we will look at bending each note one at a time.

BENDING HOLE 4

Because there's only one bend to get and because it sits comfortably in the middle of the harmonica, the 4th hole draw is the easiest hole to start bending.

Get a good clean sound on draw 4. Now try all the techniques discussed in the previous pages, such as dropping the jaw, tightening your lips around the top and bottom of the harmonica and singing into it; anything which might deflect the air coming across the reed.

Once you get the bend and you understand the technique for achieving it, try playing it over and over: woo woo woo.

Next you must learn to hold the bend down for as long as possible This will give you great strength in the jaw and train your facial muscles to hold the necessary shape.

Practise the following exercises until you are comfortable bending.

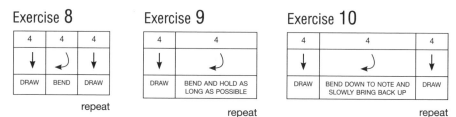

Practise these bending exercises until you have them under complete control. On a C harp this bent note is the C# note.

If you refer to the chart on page 13, you will see that the 4th hole draw is a D note and the 4th hole blow is a C note. On the chromatic chart on page 8, the only note between them is the C# and now you know how to get that note on a diatonic harp through the magic of bending. In the key of G (remember, this is the key we are playing in on our C harmonica), this note is the very bluesy sounding flattened fifth.

When you have this hole under control, it's time to move on to hole one.

BENDING HOLE 1

B ecause it is the longest of the draw reeds, the number one bend requires the most strength. Like hole number four, there is only one bend on the first hole draw. It is the same note as that on hole number four except it is an octave lower.

All the techniques you have employed to bend hole number four need to be used for the number one bend: you have to really tighten up your jaw and bite down hard on the harp.

If you are having trouble bending this hole, or just bending in general, try this trick with your nose. The nostrils are open and relaxed when playing unbent notes. When you are bending, however, the nostrils are tightened and almost pinched closed, which changes the air stream flow and contributes to the bend, allowing it to happen.

Draw on hole four cleanly, and then suck air through your nostrils as well as your mouth. Pinch your nostrils closed with your free hand. You will feel the pressure build up in the back of your throat and the bend begin to happen. Once you get that feeling in your throat, you'll know the sensation you're trying to achieve with every bend.

Again, you must hold the bend down for as long as possible. This will strengthen the jaw and train the facial muscles to hold the shape necessary for the first hole bend, which takes the most strength of all the notes on the harmonica. Here are the same exercises as the draw 4 bend on hole 1.

Exercise 11

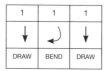

repeat

Exercise 12

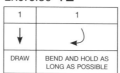

repeat

Exercise 13

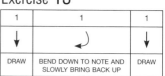

repeat

Practise these bending exercises until you have them under complete control. On a C harp, this bent note is the C# note. If you refer to the chart on page 13, you will see that the 1st hole draw is a D note and the 1st hole blow is a C note. On the chromatic chart on page 8, the only note between them is the C#, which as we know from our fourth hole study is the bluesy flattened fifth. Compare these two notes with the two notes on the fourth hole and you will see that they are the same notes on hole 1 except they are an octave apart.

Try this exercise: play a clean note on hole 1, and then play the bent note on hole 1. Now play a clean note on hole 4, and then the bent note on the hole 4. Alternate back and forth between the two holes.

Exercise 14

1	1	1	4	4	4
↓	↩	↓	↓	↩	↓
DRAW	BEND	DRAW	DRAW	BEND	DRAW

repeat

This is a good exercise to develop single note accuracy. You don't want any spill-over from holes 2 and 3; you just want to play holes 4 and 1.

BENDING HOLE 6

The sixth hole draw has only one bend, just like hole 1 and hole 4. Refer to the chart on page 13 and you'll see that the note of the six hole blow is a G and the draw note is an A. If you refer to page 25, you'll notice that the missing note between these two is G# (or A♭ depending on how you choose to refer to it.) That's why there is only one bend on the first, fourth and sixth holes, because chromatically there's only one note that we can play between those blow and draw notes.

Because the reed of the sixth hole draw is lighter and shorter than the reeds on holes 1 and 4, it is much easier to bend. All of the practising you have been doing on holes 1 and 4 should make your jaw and facial muscles strong enough to really wail on the hole six draw.

Use the same exercises that you have been playing for holes 1 and 4 draw, this time on the sixth hole. Here are the exercises again:

Exercise 15

6	6	6
↓	↵	↓
DRAW	BEND	DRAW

repeat

Exercise 16

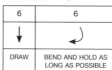

6	6
↓	↵
DRAW	BEND AND HOLD AS LONG AS POSSIBLE

repeat

Exercise 17

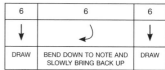

6	6	6
↓	↵	↓
DRAW	BEND DOWN TO NOTE AND SLOWLY BRING BACK UP	DRAW

repeat

We can also now expand exercise 14 to include hole 6. It won't sound very musical but it's a great way to practise your single note accuracy as well as your bending technique.

Exercise 18

1	1	1	4	4	4	6	6	6
↓	↵	↓	↓	↵	↓	↓	↵	↓
DRAW	BEND	DRAW	DRAW	BEND	DRAW	DRAW	BEND	DRAW

repeat

Exercise 18 begins on the straight note and goes down to the bend, but you can also practise it the other way around, from the bent note coming up to the straight note. This is much more difficult to achieve and much more difficult to control.

Exercise 19

4	4	1	1	6	6
↵	↓	↵	↓	↵	↓
BEND	DRAW	BEND	DRAW	BEND	DRAW

repeat

Exercise 20

1	1	4	4	6	6
↵	↓	↵	↓	↵	↓
BEND	DRAW	BEND	DRAW	BEND	DRAW

repeat

You must hit the bent note as accurately as possible. Don't bend down to the note – just hit it already bent. This is very tough!

These bending exercises might seem boring and repetitive, but you are slowly building the technical requirements that are absolutely necessary to become a great harmonica player.

Practice can be very tedious. It is natural to want to get out there and just blow, but you can't build a whole house unless you know how to lay a single brick, and that's what we're doing now – building the foundation.

Now that you've got holes 1, 4 and 6 under control, it's time to move on to the two holes that have multiple – and therefore more difficult – bends.

BENDING HOLE 2

So far you've studied the holes which have only one bend. But if you refer to the charts on pages 8 and 25, you will see that between the draw 2 (a G note) and the blow 2 (an E note), there are two other notes – an F# and an F natural. Both of these notes can be obtained by subtle and accurate bending.

THE FULL BEND ON HOLE 2

The first bend we will look at on hole 2 is the F natural. This is as low as this hole can be bent. It is the blues seventh – the flattened seventh – and is an essential note in the blues. It requires some strength and power to achieve and hold this bend. It is notated like this:

 The two slashes indicate that this is the 2nd or full bend on hole 2.

First play a long, clear, single note on draw 2. If you still cannot get a clean single note without some of the other holes bleeding into the sound, then go back to the early chapters and work on your single note technique. Single notes and the art of bending are completely intertwined techniques and you will not be able to bend without being able to achieve a clean single note. Be honest with yourself – if you know you are not achieving a clear, clean sound then go back and do the work needed to make it happen.

If you are not getting a clean sound but are getting a sort of strangulated choke sound, it's because you may be already semi-bending the reed. This is because when you are puckering up and sucking in the air, you are slightly closing off your nostrils. This causes the pressure to build up in the back of the mouth cavity and leads to a sort of half bent, honking sound. Whilst this is not a good thing, it does show you how the art of bending can be achieved.

If this is happening to you, remind yourself how to achieve a single note. Blow and draw on holes 1, 2, 3 and 4. This will remind you of the sensation of air simply flowing, unbent, through the harmonica. Then go back to an unbent pucker-up, with the same sensation of air flowing cleanly through the harp.

Now that we've revised, let's get a big blues bend happening.

Make a clean note, and then suck that bend down as hard as you can and hold it down until your lungs are bursting.

Here are the same exercises we used on holes 1, 4 and 6:

Exercise 21

2	2	2
↓	↲	↓
DRAW	BEND	DRAW

repeat

Exercise 22

2	2
↓	↲
DRAW	BEND AND HOLD AS LONG AS POSSIBLE

repeat

Exercise 23

2	2	2
↓	↲	↓
DRAW	BEND DOWN TO NOTE AND SLOWLY BRING BACK UP	DRAW

repeat

THE HALF BEND ON HOLE 2

The other bend you can achieve on hole 2 is the half bend – the F#. In the key of G, which, remember, you are playing in on a C harp, the F# is called the major seventh. This is a very sweet sounding note and is rarely used in blues playing. However, in some country music and in a jazz setting it is a necessary bend to have in your repertoire.

To achieve this bend, hold a clear draw 2 and then slowly bend down to the full bend, the blues bend.

On the way down to that note, you will pass the major seventh. Now try it again, but this time stop halfway when you reach F# and try to hold that bend in place. It's very difficult and the note tends to warble a bit between the full and half bend. Persevere and you will be able to control this.

A good exercise is to start on the full bend and bring it up to the half bend and then to the clean draw, holding each part of the bend for a few seconds.

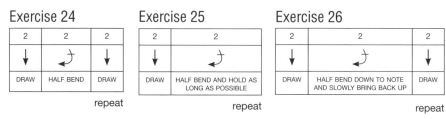

Exercise 24

2	2	2
DRAW	HALF BEND	DRAW

repeat

Exercise 25

2	2
DRAW	HALF BEND AND HOLD AS LONG AS POSSIBLE

repeat

Exercise 26

2	2	2
DRAW	HALF BEND DOWN TO NOTE AND SLOWLY BRING BACK UP	DRAW

repeat

Exercise 27

2	2	2	2	2
DRAW	HALF BEND	FULL BEND	HALF BEND	DRAW

repeat

Move down through the two bends and back up again.

BENDING HOLE 3

From the chart on page 13, you can see that the clean draw 3 is a B note. In the key of G major this is the third note of the scale. It's a tricky note to handle in the blues. What makes the blues work is that even though it is in a major key, the third is usually flattened like a minor. This, along with the similarly flattened seventh note of the scale, gives the blues the dissonance (the distinctive clashing notes) that makes it work. This doesn't occur in country-style where the third is sweetly major.

You will see from the chart on page 25 that there are 3 notes missing between the draw 3 (B) and the blow 3 (G). Those notes are B♭, A and A♭. Let's get bending.

Unlike the second hole, where we learned to bend the reed to its lowest point and then come up slowly to get the half bend, this time we are going to gently bend down through the three bends on the third hole.

THE FIRST BEND ON HOLE 3

Once again, begin with a clean tone, and then gently begin to bend. Just lightly moving your tongue into the bending position should help you achieve this bend. It is very important to get this first bend right. You are flattening the major third (B) into the minor or blues flattened third (B♭).

A lot of beginners (and a lot of professionals for that matter) don't handle this bend correctly. It is easy to bend the note too far into one of the other bends on this hole. This makes the note sound either out of tune or just plain wrong.

Exercise 28

3	3	3
↓	↴	↓
DRAW	FIRST BEND	DRAW

repeat

Hold the first bend for as long as possible before bringing it up to the straight draw position.

THE SECOND BEND ON HOLE 3

Slowly bend down through the first bend to the next half bend. This note is an A. In the G scale, this is the second note. It is rarely used in the blues but you will definitely use it country music, especially when playing a melody (playing the actual tune).

This exercise will help you practise the first two bends on this hole.

Next, try this variation.

Exercise 29

3	3	3
↓	↲♪	↲⹁
DRAW	FIRST BEND	SECOND BEND

repeat

Exercise 30

3	3	3	3	3
↓	↲♪	↲⹁	↲♪	↓
DRAW	FIRST BEND	SECOND BEND	FIRST BEND	DRAW

repeat

This sort of control is very difficult and can drive you mad (I speak from experience!), so don't think you are alone if you are having trouble with the subtleties of this third hole.

THE THIRD BEND ON HOLE 3

The third hole can be bent again down to the A♭. You will almost never need to play this note. In the scale of G it is called a flattened 9th (or 2nd). It is the second note of the scale (A), flattened a semitone. You may get to use it in a jazz setting but very rarely otherwise.

Nevertheless, you have to be able to control the bend because understanding how it feels to bend down to this note will help distinguish between the three subtle bends on this hole.

Once again, start with a straight clean note and slowly bend down through the semitones on bends 1 and 2. Keep bending until you get the next note down.

Exercise 31

3	3	3	3
↓	↲♪	↲⹁	↲⹁
DRAW	FIRST BEND	SECOND BEND	THIRD (FULL) BEND

repeat

Again, hold each subtle bend as long as possible.

In this exercise we go down through the bends and then back up again.

Exercise 32

3	3	3	3	3	3	3
↓	↙	↙	↙	↙	↙	↓
DRAW	FIRST BEND	SECOND BEND	THIRD BEND	SECOND BEND	FIRST BEND	DRAW

repeat

When playing the country-style harp, the third note is usually played straight, without much bending. However, to add some style to your playing, you can 'scoop' up to the clean note by slightly bending up to the note. This little riff demonstrates this well.

Exercise 33

First with no 'scoop'.

1	2	2	3
↓	↑	↓	↓
DRAW	BLOW	DRAW	DRAW

repeat

By slightly 'scooping' up to the note, the riff has more character.

1	2	2	3
↓	↑	↓	⊻
DRAW	BLOW	DRAW	SCOOP UP

repeat

The little '‿' above the note indicates to scoop up to the clean note.

A great exercise to cement the sound of the second and third hole bends in your mind is to play a major scale from blow 1.

A C major scale is automatically produced from the blow 4 on the C harmonica like this:

Exercise 34

4	4	5	5	6	6	7	7
↑	↓	↑	↓	↑	↓	↓	↑
BLOW	DRAW	BLOW	DRAW	BLOW	DRAW	DRAW	BLOW

repeat

When played from hole blow 1, the C major scale requires real control of your bends.

Exercise 35

1	1	2	2	2	3	3	4
↑	↓	↑	↙	↓	↙	↓	↑
BLOW	DRAW	BLOW	FULL BEND	DRAW	SECOND BEND	DRAW	BLOW

repeat

Play this C major scale exercise ascending and descending.

TONGUING

Grab your harp and play a long pure single note on blow 3. Yes that's right, I said *blow*, not *draw*.

While playing the blow 3, say 'ta'. The tip of your tongue will touch the ridge behind your top teeth. By now you will have realised that blow 3 and draw 2 give you the same note. This is the **tonic** or **key note** in the cross harp. On a C harp, this is the key note of G. (I always use the draw 2 as the tonic note rather than the blow 3, because the draw notes are more easily 'coloured' by bending).

Play blow 3 and say 'ta' and then 'ta ta' and 'ta ta ta' etc, in any combination you like. This 'ta ta' stops the air flowing into or through the harp, thereby stopping and starting the note. Saxophone and trumpet players call this 'articulation' and it works like the punctuation in a sentence, giving rhythmic sense to your playing and greater control over your sound.

The 'ta ta' technique is quite easy on the blow notes because it's similar to talking. However, you must learn the technique on the draw notes. This is much more difficult because you are sucking air into the harp and saying 'ta ta' at the same time.

Try talking while breathing in – you'll be lucky not to swallow your false teeth! The trick in both blowing and drawing is not actually to say 'ta' using your voice, but to make your tongue click, or 'tut', as if you were voicing disapproval. The tongue is a muscle and will respond to exercise by becoming stronger and more controllable, so don't be discouraged if your first attempts at tonguing the draw notes are sluggish and ragged.

Practise the 'ta' or 'tut' tonguing on every note, draw and blow, and then try different combinations of notes (e.g. draw 1, draw 2, draw 2, draw 4, draw 3, draw 6), articulating each note. Make up any combinations you like, mixing up draw and blow notes, making sure you always hit clear, single notes. Here are two exercises to practise this.

Exercise 36

1	2	3	4	3	2	1
↓	↓	↓	↓	↓	↓	↓
TA	TA	TA	TA	TA	TA	TA

repeat

Exercise 37

1	2	3	4
↓	↓	↓	↓
TA TA TA	TA TA TA	TA TA TA	TA TA TA

repeat

Another tonguing device is to say 'tidderly, tidderly' over and over. This creates a rolling type of articulation. Try it with this exercise:

Exercise 38

1	2	3	4	3	2	1
↓	↓	↓	↓	↓	↓	↓
TIDDERLY	TIDDERLY	TIDDERLY	TIDDERLY	TIDDERLY	TIDDERLY	TIDDERLY

repeat

You will find that when practising these techniques, your command over single notes and your overall sound will automatically improve. Once you get going, learning an instrument has a snowball effect – each new thing you learn reinforces the preceding exercises.

VIBRATO

When a singer sings or when you hear a flute or saxophone player, you will have noticed that the notes (especially the long notes) begin to warble towards the end. This is called vibrato (meaning vibration).

Singers do it by moving their larynx up and down, guitarists do it by moving their fingers up and down on the string and saxophone players do it by releasing and tightening their bottom lip. Harp players have a wide variety of techniques available to produce vibrato: the hands, larynx or tongue, or any combination, produce totally different kinds of vibrato.

HAND CUPPING

The hand cupping technique is the easiest and most common. With your free hand, just basically flap away. Don't do it for the entire note and don't do it on every note. Introduce it towards the end of a long note. Use small movements with the hand barely moving right through to whole arm movements for a wild sound.

Practise making a very tight cup with your hand to completely choke off the sound. This is the 'cry baby' trick.

You can also flap your hand. This creates a 'chorus' sound.

The tongue dart

Some players achieve a vibrato by making the tongue dart in and out. They play a note and just move their tongue back and forth. It is difficult to do when bending, and the effect is a bit corny.

The glottal stop

I think the best vibrato is achieved by employing the glottal stop. This works particularly well on the draw notes and has a very vocal quality. To get this kind of vibrato, use your epiglottis: the little flap of skin at the back of the throat that covers your windpipe when you swallow.

An easier way to understand this is to be a kookaburra! That noise you've tried to make when you want to emulate a kookaburra is exactly the same process as the glottal stop. You are making an 'oo oo oo' sound whilst sucking in air.

The advantage of this kind of vibrato is that it can be very finely controlled with greater subtlety than the other vibratos and is very effective if you are playing amplified harp and can't use your cupping hand.

Rhythm playing

The harp is a great instrument for rhythm playing. If you're having a bit of trouble getting some of the single note and bending techniques under control, have some fun with one of the easiest tricks to achieve – the lonesome train. We will slowly get the train up to speed and then bring it into the station – all with our mouths wide open, playing just about any old note!

Exercise 39

1 Exhale all the air from your lungs.

2 Draw on holes 2 and 3 and say 'ta ta'.

3 Blow into the same holes and say 'ta ta'.

4 Draw on 1 and 2 and say 'ta ta'.

5 Blow 2 and 3 and say 'ta ta'.

6 Repeat over and over.

Here it is written out:

2 – 3	2 – 3	1 – 2	2 – 3
↓	↑	↓	↑
DRAW	BLOW	DRAW	BLOW
TA TA	TA TA	TA TA	TA TA

repeat

This produces the basic chugging rhythm of the train sound.

Once you have established the chugging of the train, it's time to add a few effects. When you feel like the train is at the station, take a big draw on holes 4 and 5. This is the lonesome wailing train cry. Try different cupping and fanning techniques with your right hand. It's a wild sound isn't it?

We can make it better by trying it this way:

1 Start on a clean, unbent 4 hole draw.

2 Bend it down.

3 When you bring it back up to the clean draw note, open up your mouth and allow the draw 5 and the draw 4 to sound together.

4 Use your hand to get a 'woo woo' sound happening.

Also try bending both 4 and 5 notes together. This takes a lot of strength, because the 5 hole doesn't have a missing note to bend to, so it resists the bend and sounds like it's going to snap, producing a great sound.

		RAPID RIP TO		
4	4/5	4	3	2
↓	↓	↓	↓	↓
DRAW	DRAW	DRAW	DRAW	DRAW

repeat

BLUES-STYLE HARP

Although there are literally hundreds of different types of chord progressions that can make up the blues, there is one standard format: the 12 bar blues. It's the simplest form of the blues, and is made up of three basic chords.

What is a chord? Here is the G major scale:

A chord is made up of alternate thirds. Take the first note (G) and go to the third note (B). Then go up another third to the D note.

G, B and D are also the three notes you get when you draw on holes 2, 3 and 4 on the C harp. That's why cross harp works.

Start on the 4th note of the scale (C), go up a third to the E and up again to G. C, E and G: that's a C chord.

Do the same thing from the 5th note of the scale (D) and you get a D chord.

Simple, isn't it? G, C and D chords are the three basic chords of the 12 bar blues.

Here are some standard blues tricks and licks:

Lick 1

4	5	4	5
↓	↓	↓	↓
DRAW	DRAW	DRAW	DRAW

repeat

The four and five hole shake.
Draw on hole 4, then move your head to hole 5. Go back and forth to create a 'blues shake'. Some people move the harp back and forth with their free hand, but this is not as subtle or easy as the head shake. You can also bend the shake up and down.

Lick 2

4	4	4	3	2
↪	↓	↪	↓	↓
BEND	DRAW	BEND	DRAW	END ON DRAW 2

repeat

Lick 3

4	4	5	2
↪	↓	↓	↓
BEND	DRAW	DRAW	END ON DRAW 2

repeat

Lick 4

2	2 – 3 – 4	3	2	2	2
↓	↑	↩	↓	↩	↓
DRAW	BLOW	FIRST BEND	DRAW	FULL BEND	DRAW

repeat

Lick 5

3/4	4/5	4/5	4/5	3/4
↓	↑	↓	↑	↓
DRAW SHAKE	BLOW SHAKE	DRAW SHAKE	BLOW SHAKE	END ON DRAW SHAKE 3/4

repeat

Lick 6

6	5	4	4	4	3	2
↑	↓	↓	↩	↑	↩	↓
BLOW	DRAW	DRAW	BEND	BLOW	FIRST BEND	DRAW

repeat

COUNTRY-STYLE HARP

Country-style harmonica playing uses all of the puckering and bending techniques that are used for the blues but with a few vital variations.

If you draw on hole number five when playing the blues, you get the dissonant note: a flattened 7th. Playing the full bend on draw 2 also gives you this dissonant note, but an octave lower. It's this dissonance which makes the blues sound like the blues.

Most of the time in country music, this note will sound wrong. So instead of drawing on hole 5 and using the full draw 2 bend, we blow these holes.

When you blow hole number 2 and hole number 5, the note you get is the 6th note of the scale. In the key of G, this is an E note, a beautiful note.

The three chords of the blues are also used in country songs. There are also lots of country songs with more complicated chord structures but most of the 'other' chords will have come from the same alternate thirds method of chord construction, like this.

If you build a chord from:
- the 2nd note of the G scale, you get an A minor chord.
- the 3rd note of the G scale, you get a B minor chord.
- the 6th note of the G scale, you get an E minor chord.

The blow 2 and blow 5 can be played across any of these chords.

Here are some country licks and tricks:

Lick 1

3	4	3	4
↓	↓	↓	↓
DRAW	DRAW	DRAW	DRAW

repeat

The 3 and 4 draw shake.

This is performed just like the first blues lick on page 47, by moving your head between the notes.

Lick 2

3	4	3	3	2	3
⌄	↓	↓	↩	↓	⌄
SCOOP TO DRAW	DRAW	DRAW	FIRST BEND	DRAW	SCOOP UP

repeat

Lick 3

3	4	3	3	2	2	1	2
⌄	↓	↓	↩	↓	↑	↓	↓
SCOOP TO DRAW	DRAW	DRAW	FIRST BEND	DRAW	BLOW	DRAW	DRAW

repeat

Lick 4

3	4	3	4	3	2
⌄	↓	⌄	↓	⌄	↓
SCOOP TO DRAW	DRAW	SCOOP	DRAW	SCOOP	END ON DRAW 2

repeat

Lick 5

1	2	2	3	4	5	4	6
↓	↑	↓	⌄	↓	↑	↓	↑
DRAW	BLOW	DRAW	SCOOP TO DRAW	DRAW	BLOW	DRAW	BLOW

repeat

Lick 6

6	5	5	4	5	4	3	3	2
↑	↑	↓	↓	↑	↓	↓	↩	↓
BLOW	BLOW	DRAW	DRAW	BLOW	DRAW	DRAW	FIRST BEND	DRAW

repeat

AMPLIFIED HARP

I n most performance settings, the harp needs to be amplified in order to be heard above the din of the other instruments in the band.

Amplifying harmonicas started in the late forties when, in the post-war economic boom, amplifiers for guitars and bass became more readily available to the public. This started a general increase in the volume level of music which continues unabated today.

The harp stylists of that era, like Walter Horton and Little Walter Jacobs, began playing harp into cheap microphones through cheap amplifiers. This led to the swooping, reverberated, distorted sound which we now recognise and hear so often.

AMP AND MIKE COMBINATIONS

For the aspiring harp player looking to amplify their harp and sound, there are thousands of amp and mike combinations.

For a microphone, you can use virtually anything. I alternate between using a vocal mike straight through the P.A. system, a little saxophone bug or lapel mike, also through the P.A. system, and a mike through a 10-watt amp for studio sessions where sound but not volume is important.

Harmonica microphones can be heavy and cumbersome. Some are also inconvenient with no on/off switch, which leads to feedback (an ear-splitting, whistling sound). They can also be expensive: don't use a $500 microphone to amplify a $50 harp.

vocal mikes

saxophone
bug/lapel mi.

amplifier

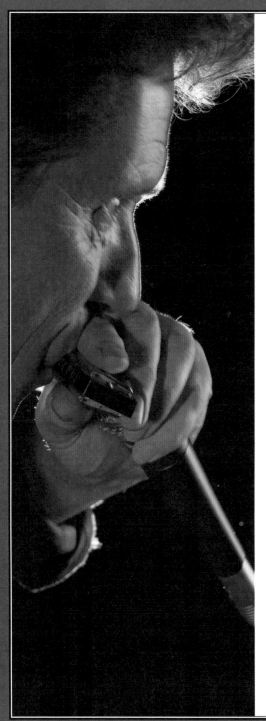

If you are playing straight into a vocal mike, make sure you have the monitor level low enough so you can completely cup the harp and mike without feedback. In fact, just about any microphone will serve to give your sound the edge and distortion required as the close proximity of the harp to the mike's diaphragm creates natural distortion.

You can also buy ready-amplified harmonicas. These come with microphones built in to the harmonica and a hole to put the lead in. Just plug the lead straight into the harmonica and the P.A. system.

amplified harmonica

Over the years, I have used various setups on stage. I've used a cheap mike through a 40-watt amp or an electronic distortion and booster pedal straight into the P.A. system. Currently I either go straight through a vocal mike into the P.A. (for country or jazz style playing) or play through a sax bug (if I need a distorted blues sound).

These days I only use an amp in the studio, and in fact I've never liked having to carry big amps around. If you want to get a big amp, there are hundreds to choose from, but try to get one with reverb and distortion knobs.

For the home or garage, a simple 10 watt amp and any old mike will do the job. To play with a loud band, you'll need at least 60 watts and probably 100 watts to be heard. Amps of this size, no matter what make, will cost a lot of money.

DISTORTION

Modern technology gives us an array of devices which can give you all the distortion, edge and reverb that you need. Because they plug straight into the P.A. system, you can leave the volume decisions in the hands of a sound engineer.

To create distortion, you can use something as simple as an analogue distortion pedal or a variety of pedals, such as chorus, delay, etc., slaved together.

A better alternative is to use one of the multi-effects units now available. Apart from the regular harp effects, you can use harmonising effects to play octaves along with yourself so that you sound like a harp section.

distortion pedal

You can also use a loop station. This allows you to play a lick (such as the train rhythm), which the loop station then plays back over and over while you play other licks across the top. Who needs a guitarist!

THIRD POSITION – THE MINOR SOUND

It's time to look at the concept of third position harp. To refresh your memory, remember that:

- **first position** means playing a harp in the same key as the band.
- **second position** is the traditional blues position cross harp where you play the harp of the 4th note of the scale (i.e. the key of G, cross harp C).

Third position is also known as double cross harp, which means that you 'cross' twice to get the right harp.

For example, if the band is in G, count up 4 (G, A, B, C) to get to cross harp (or second) position – a C harp.

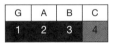

Then count up 4 again (C, D, E, F) to get to third position – an F harp. So to play third position in the key of G, use an F harp.

So, for example, to play in the key of A, a G harp can be used. Another way of determining which harp to use for third position is to ask the guitarist you're playing with what is the flattened seventh in the key he is playing. In the key of A, G is the flattened seventh.

Here is a list of some keys with cross and double cross harps to use.

KEY (FIRST POSITION)	CROSS HARP (SECOND POSITION)	DOUBLE CROSS (THIRD POSITION)
A	D	G
G	C	F
C	F	B♭
D	G	C
E	A	D
F	B♭	E♭

Of course you can't play double cross harp the same way as ordinary cross harp because the notes are in different positions. So what notes do you play? The tonic, or key note, which is found on draw 2 in cross harp, is draw 1 and 4 in 3rd position. This means that in certain keys the range you are playing is drastically different.

For example, in the key of A, the normal cross harp, D, is one of the higher pitched harps, but by using double cross with the lowest pitched harp, the G, your tonic note is an octave lower.

The advantages of occasionally playing 3rd position are that your range is altered and you can impose a definite minor sound to the blues, which is usually caught somewhat ambiguously between the major and minor tonalities.

Pick a song on a record that you know the key of and experiment with 3rd position. You will find that your 'wailing note' is now on draw 6 rather than draw 4, and virtually all the notes which sit comfortably with the key are draw notes. By drawing at the high end of the harp on any group of notes, you form a minor chord. This can be hauntingly effective on a slow blues.

In order to use the C harmonica in the third position, you have to play in the key of D. D crosses to G which crosses to C: the double cross!

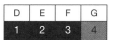 

So to practise your third position, ask a guitarist to play a minor blues in D (cross to G, then cross again to C) and wail away on your C harp.

TONGUE BLOCKING

So far, you've been puckering up. Forget all that: now it's time to tongue block.

This technique involves opening up the mouth and playing 4 or sometimes 5 holes at once. For example, draw on notes 1, 2, 3 and 4. Then place the tip of your tongue on holes 2 and 3, like this:

Now the only holes that are sounding are the 1 and 4 holes. The chart on page 13 tells us that on the C harp, the 1 and 4 draws are D notes, an octave apart. The harp is beautifully set up to play octaves.

The tongue block can be used for drawing and blowing. If you open up hole 3, 4, 5 and 6 blows and then put your tongue on holes 4 and 5, you are left with blow 3 and 6. This is the G, or tonic note, in the key of G, and this is one of the rare times that you will use the blow 3 rather than the draw 2 to get the tonic note.

The chart below shows all the octave combinations you can achieve with tongue blocking. The blocked holes are in brackets.

Blow 1 (2, 3) 4 = C octaves
Draw 1 (2, 3) 4 = D octaves
Blow 2 (3, 4) 5 = E octaves
Blow 3 (4, 5) 6 = G octaves
Blow 4 (5, 6) 7 = C octaves
Blow 6 (7, 8) 9 = G octaves
Draw 4 (5, 6, 7) 8 = D octaves
Draw 3 (4, 5, 6) 7 = B octaves

This technique can be used to make a fantastic accordion sound. By slipping between the pucker up and the tongue block, you can achieve the chugging sound of the accordion and add great propulsion to your rhythm playing.

Here are all the tongue block options:

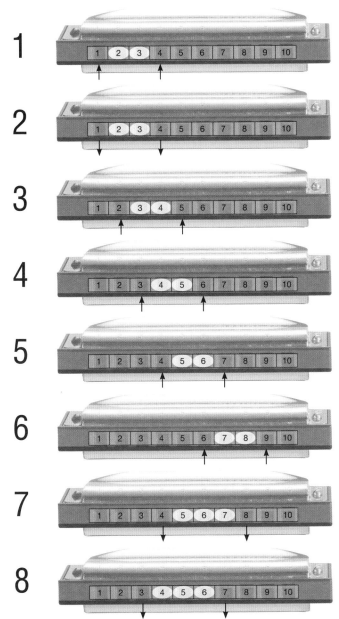

COPYING SOLOS

The best way to learn tunes and licks is not to read them from a book but to emulate what you hear on record. Officially it's called transcribing. Take your favourite licks and, using the fundamentals you have learned, try to work out the solo note for note. That way, you are learning from the masters. Don't be afraid of sounding like someone else; your own style will emerge as you learn.

When I was learning, I discovered that an LP record that revolved at 33 rpm could be slowed down to 16 rpm on the turntable. This meant the solos came out at half speed. Of course, it completely destroyed the record, but it meant that you could hear a solo played really slowly. Unfortunately, it was also an octave lower and very muddy, but it was a perfect way to work out every nuance of a solo and it was great for training the ears.

These days, for hardly any money at all, you can buy transcribing software on the internet. Put in the solo you want to learn and you can slow it down to any speed you like, without altering the pitch. It's just like having a teacher in the room with you, slowly showing what to do. I highly recommend that you get yourself some of this software. You'll be amazed at how much you can learn and how much your playing will improve if you learn just one or two solos perfectly.

I learned the blues when I was a teenager by mostly studying just one record. It was called *Chicago Blues* by John Young with Walter Horton on the harmonica. I learned every single note on that record: every lick, every nuance. To this day, I can still play every solo on that battered old record. It took about a year to learn the entire record but the difference it made to my playing was the difference between being an amateur and being professionally ready for any gig.

When I was 19, I studied about twenty Charlie McCoy tunes. This formed the basis of my country style. That effort to learn Walter Horton and Charlie McCoy still makes my playing sound how it does now, so get copying!

STAGECRAFT

When you have some basic harmonica techniques together, you will probably want to get up and have a bit of a jam with a band or with some musician friends.

There are some basic rules of etiquette when having a jam with other players. Over the years, lots of different players have asked me if they can get up on stage and have a jam with me. I always encourage it, because I might learn something! However, some players, possibly because of nerves, completely overplay, filling up every little gap with their squawking and playing over the top of the singing or other people's solos. If you do that, you probably won't be asked back by that band.

It's better to hang back and let the tune unfold. Solo when you are invited to. Never play across the singer. Instead, fill in the little gaps between the words with some tasty licks. Don't go flying in and showing off all your tricks in the first few seconds. Take the time to build your solo and take it to a climax at the end. Don't peak at the beginning – you'll have nowhere to go!

Be careful not to cause feedback by cupping the vocal mike too hard. Check the mike's sensitivity and back off if you hear a whistling sound. The sound guy will fix it. Above all, show respect to your fellow musos. We're all in this together!

FAQ

Q. If a reed breaks on my harmonica, can I replace it?

A. Some of the harmonica companies make replaceable reed plates, but they cost just about as much as a new harmonica and you have to do all the fiddling around with the screws. Because the harmonica is a relatively cheap instrument, it's easier to buy a new one.

Q. Who did you listen to when you were learning?

A. I first got interested in the sound of the harmonica when John Lennon played it in The Beatles. By the time I was about 17, I had started finding out about the blues. From then until now, my favourite blues harmonica player was Walter Horton. I also love the playing of Little Walter Jacobs, Paul Butterfield, Charlie Musselwhite and Sonny Boy Williamson.

My favourite country player, in fact my favourite harmonica player of all, is the great Charlie McCoy. All of his albums are available on CD, and no matter whether you are interested in the blues or country style, Charlie McCoy has the finest technique of any harmonica player I have ever heard. I also love the playing of Norton Buffalo and Howard Levy.

Q. How long did it take you to learn?

A. When you are young, you don't really start out with a goal of achieving something or actually getting somewhere. I was about 13 when I got interested in the harmonica. I just wanted to make the sounds. When you are young, you don't really notice how long it's taking you to learn something – you just want to do it. But you never stop learning and refining your technique.

However, I also play the saxophone, which I didn't take up until I was 24 years old. I had to fit learning the instrument into and around a regular working life, so I know how difficult that can be.

The best advice I can give is to say that any time that you put the harmonica in your mouth is time well spent. It doesn't matter if it's only ten minutes or ten seconds. As long as you start playing, you will find yourself playing a bit more than you may have intended. The hardest part is starting. Keep a harmonica in your pocket. Play in the car when you're waiting for the lights to change. Sit in the backyard and play. At night, turn off the lights and play in the dark, concentrating on the pure sound. Wherever you can: practise!

Q. How can I work out which harp to use if I am playing along with a recording and there's no band to ask what key they're playing in?

A. The first chord of the blues is almost always the tonic chord. The tonic chord is the key you are in.

So in a G blues, the first chord is a G chord. The first note of the G chord is a G. This is the key centre or tonic note. The tonic note is on draw 2 on the harp. So, play through your various harps until the draw 2 sounds the same as the tonic note.

Your tonal memory with soon develop and you will be able to find the key in seconds.

Q. Sometimes my harmonica sounds a bit stuffy or a reed won't work at all. What can I do?

A. The first thing you can try is to run the front and back of the harmonica under a tap. Shake out the moisture and see if the harmonica will work now. If not, get a small screwdriver and take off the cover plates. See if there's any dirt stuck on a reed. If a piece of fluff is blocking the reed, blow it out or flick it out with the screwdriver, being careful not to break the reed. If there's nothing obvious blocking the reed plate, then the reed itself is broken. It's time to get a new harp.

GLOSSARY

FLAT
A note that has been lowered by a semitone. ♭ is the symbol for a flat.

HARMONICA, HARP, FRENCH HARP, MOUTH HARP
All names for the same thing. (A country and western star I played with called Chad Morgan even called it the gob organ!)

KEY
There are twelve major scales, all built to the same formula.

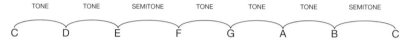

There is a major scale built on each note of the chromatic scale and there is a harp for each of these twelve keys.

MAJOR SCALE
This is the do-re-mi that everyone learned in school. You don't have to be able to play your scales to play the harmonica; you just have to know which harp fits with which key.

OCTAVE
If you play a scale (say a G scale), the difference between the first G you play and the G at the end of the scale is called an octave. Oct – as in octopus (eight arms) or octagon (eight sides) – means eight. On a piano there are eight white keys between each octave.

SHARP
A note that has been raised by a semitone. # is the symbol for a sharp.

SEMITONE
A semitone is the smallest interval in Western music. C to C# is a semitone.

TONE
A tone is made up of two semitones. The interval between C and D is a tone because it is made up of two semitones: C to C# and C# to D.

CONCLUSION

Well, you got here! If you have worked through the simple exercises, by now you should have a pretty good command of the fundamentals required for good harmonica playing.

You will have noticed that, unlike other music books, this book has no tunes to learn and not very many licks either. The object is to show you the building blocks from which all the licks are created. Knowing how the fundamentals work means that you can go and learn the tunes and licks and solos from the harp players that you like the most. Remember, it's all in the ears!

Don't be afraid to ask harp players at gigs how they are doing certain things or what kind of equipment they are using. Most musicians love to talk about themselves! And most of us love to share the knowledge we have picked up over the years.

Above all, remember to have fun!

Get blowing!

ABOUT THE AUTHOR

Initially inspired by John Lennon's harmonica playing in the Beatles, Steve Williams started playing harmonica when he was 14. His first professional performances were in country music bands in 1979, playing with Australian country music legends such as Chad Morgan, Ray Kernaghan and Merv Lowry.

During the 1980s, Steve played with countless blues, country and rock bands, as well as recording thousands of albums, movie soundtracks and TV and radio themes and jingles.

In 1990, Steve was invited to play on the John Farnham *Chain Reaction* album. He has been playing with John Farnham ever since, playing on all subsequent albums and touring Australia, Europe and Asia.

Steve has also toured the US with Olivia Newton-John and recorded *One Woman's Journey Live* with her at Donald Trump's Atlantic City Taj Mahal.

Steve is currently a member of the orchestra on the popular television program *Dancing With the Stars*.